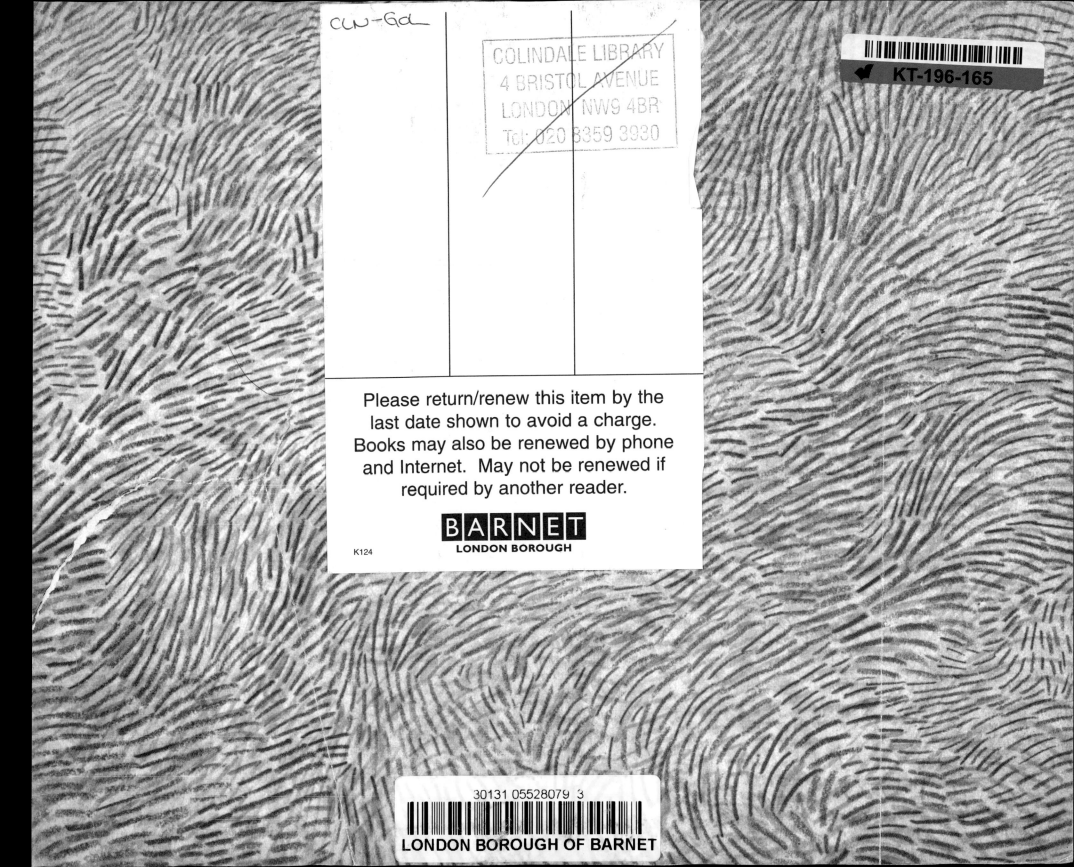

Please return/renew this item by the
last date shown to avoid a charge.
Books may also be renewed by phone
and Internet. May not be renewed if
required by another reader.

BARNET
LONDON BOROUGH

K124

THEY ALL SAW
A CAT

BRENDAN WENZEL

chronicle books · san francisco

The cat walked through the world,
with its whiskers, ears, and paws . . .

and *the child* saw A CAT,

and *the dog* saw A CAT,

and *the fox* saw A CAT.

Yes, they all saw the cat.

The cat walked through the world,

with its whiskers, ears, and paws . . .

and *the fish* saw A CAT,

and *the bee* saw A CAT.

Yes, they all saw the cat.

The cat walked through the world,

with its whiskers, ears, and paws . . .

and *the bird* saw A CAT,

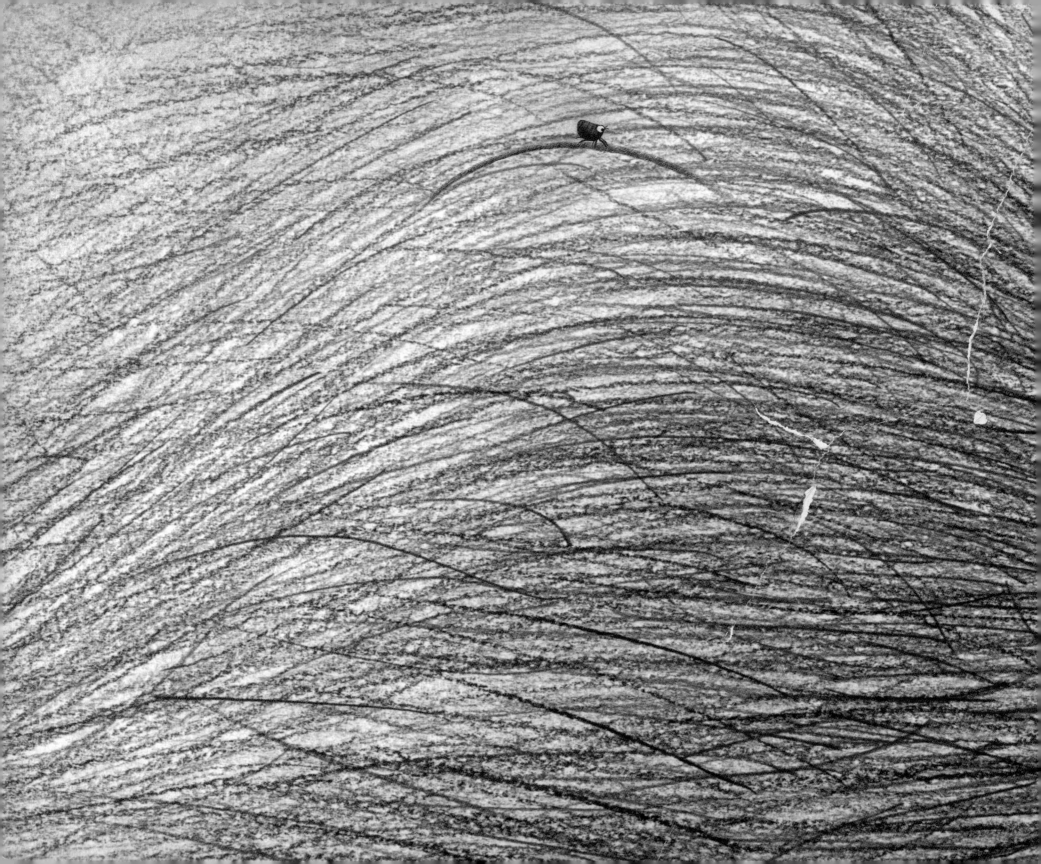

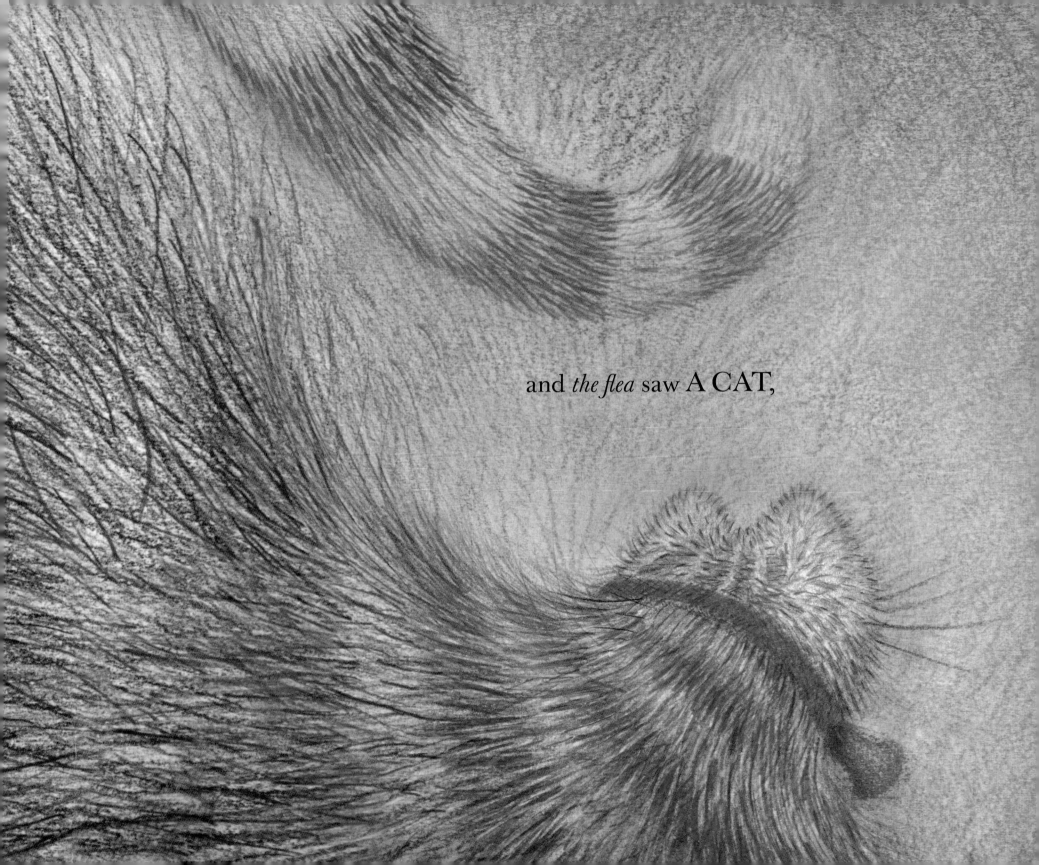

and *the flea* saw A CAT,

and *the snake* saw A CAT,

and *the skunk* saw A CAT,

and *the worm* saw A CAT,

and *the bat* saw A CAT.
Yes, they all saw the cat.

YES, THEY
ALL SAW
A CAT!

A CHILD
and A DOG
and A FOX
and A FISH
and A MOUSE
and A BEE
and A BIRD
and A FLEA
and A SNAKE
and A SKUNK
and A WORM
and A BAT.

The cat knew them all,
and they all knew the cat.

And *the cat* walked through the world,
with its whiskers, ears, and paws,

then it came to the water . . .

and imagine what it saw?

For Magdalena —B. W.

Library of Congress Cataloging-in-Publication Data:

Names: Wenzel, Brendan, author, illustrator.
Title: They all saw a cat / Brendan Wenzel.
Description: San Francisco, California : Chronicle Books, LLC, [2016] |
   Summary: In simple, rhythmic prose and stylized pictures, a cat walks through the world, and all the other creatures see and acknowledge the cat.
Identifiers: LCCN 2015045046 | ISBN 9781452150130 (alk. paper)
Subjects: LCSH: Cats—Juvenile fiction. | Identity (Psychology)—Juvenile fiction. | CYAC: Cats—Fiction. | Identity—Fiction.
Classification: LCC PZ7.1.W436 Th 2016 | DDC [E]—dc23 LC record available at http://lccn.loc.gov/2015045046

Manufactured in China.

Design by Jennifer Tolo Pierce.

Typeset in Baskerville 120 Pro.
The illustrations in this book were rendered in almost everything imaginable, including colored pencil, oil pastels, acrylic paint, watercolor, charcoal, Magic Marker, good old number 2 pencils, and even an iBook.

10 9 8 7 6 5 4 3

Chronicle Books LLC
680 Second Street
San Francisco, California 94107

Chronicle Books—we see things differently. Become part of our community at www.chroniclekids.com.